The LONG-LOST SECRET DIARY OF THE WORLD'S WORST VIKING

D1136662

First published in Great Britain by Scribo ᴍMXXı
Scribo, an imprint of
The Salariya Book Company
25 Marlborough Place, Brighton, BN1 1UB

ISBN 978-1-913971-04-5

Book design by David Salariya

Printed and bound in China

The text for this book is set in Century Schoolbook
The display type is Jacob Riley

www.salariya.com

THE LONG-LOST SECRET DIARY OF THE WORLD'S WORST VIKING

Written by
Tim Collins

Illustrated by
Isobel Lundie

SCRIBO
a SALARIYA imprint

Greenland

Route of Halfdan's
voyage

North
America

Vinland
(Newfoundland)

South
America

THE VIKING WORLD
This map shows our hero Halfdan's journey.

Iceland

Sweden

Lapland

Norway

Finland

Russia

England

Spain

Africa

Chapter *I*

Halfdan Skull-splitter

Denmark 1000 AD
First Day of the First New Moon
of Summer

Lightning will strike. Thunder will crack. Rain will fall. A scowling dragon will glide out of the ocean and frightened locals will scatter, fearing that the beast will spew fire onto their helpless village. But the truth is even more terrible.

It is not a dragon that has come to terrorise them, but a ship with a carved dragon's head. And on board are a fearsome band of raiders led by me, Halfdan Skull-splitter.

We will take all their silver and all their jewels, and we will even prise the weapons from their cold hands once they are dead.

For we are the Northmen, and we are doom.

None of this has actually happened yet, by the way. But I'm sure it will soon. I just need Dad to agree to let me go raiding. And to change my name from 'Halfdan' to 'Halfdan Skull-splitter'. And then I need Thor to provide the dramatic weather, because all we've got at the moment is light drizzle.

GET REAL

The Vikings used many imaginative nicknames to tell people with the same name apart. Examples include Thorfinn Skull-splitter, Eric Bloodaxe and Harald Hardrada, meaning 'hard-ruler'.

Second Day

Dad is refusing to let me change my name to
Halfdan Skull-splitter. He says he'll change it
to Halfdan Annoying-moaner if I ask again.

He was carving wood in the shipyard opposite
our house, and he gave me the same talk I've
heard a hundred times before. He said that
building ships is just as important as raiding.
Our great ships are the reason we can cross
seas and sail down rivers and grab exciting
things from weaker folk.

He advised me to spend more time learning
how to craft wood, and less time pretending to
be a raider. That way I'll have something to fall
back on if the raiding doesn't work out.

I'll never need anything to fall back on. I
will surge forever onward, swinging my axe,

and hacking through wood, flesh, bone and whatever stands in the way of my plunder.

At least I would if I had an axe. Dad won't let me have one in case I cut myself.

Third Day

Forget what I said. I do have an axe now. Sort of.

I met my best friend Astrid to play at raiding, and she brought one from her dad's workshop. He's the best blacksmith in our village, and he makes amazing shields and weapons.

We went to the forest north of our village and took turns playing with the axe. I pretended I was in a raid and all the trees were terrified locals. I ran towards them, roaring and swinging my axe, then I planted it right into

the bark, and gathered some twigs, which I imagined were precious jewels.

I have to admit that Astrid was faster than me, and she didn't miss the tree with the axe as much, but my roar was louder, so we both proved ourselves worthy.

I told Astrid about how Dad wants me to be a shipbuilder instead of a raider, and she said that when she's older she probably won't have a job at all. She'll just have to gather fruit and berries, bake bread and mend clothes. That sounds even more boring than making ships.

Astrid wants to be a raider too. And she's convinced it's going to come true because she looked up into the night sky and asked Thor if she should become one, and he answered with a huge clap of thunder that sounded like the word 'YES'. But even if the thunder had sounded exactly like 'NO! STICK TO THE HOUSEWORK!' it wouldn't have put her off. She's even more determined than me.

We played all day until I got exhausted and accidentally cut my leg with the axe. I've wrapped the wound in a spare tunic and gone to bed early so Dad can't gloat about how right he was.

GET REAL

In Viking society, men were traditionally expected to be hunters, fighters and traders, whilst women looked after their children and homes. But Viking women had more freedom than in many other societies at the time. They could own property and get divorced, run farms whilst their husbands were away battling or trading, and even take over permanently if their husbands died.

Fourth Day

I'm so glad the days are getting longer again.
All those evenings in our house, wrapped in a
blanket and watching the fire get very boring.

Mum and Dad have never been raiding, so they
don't have any exciting stories to tell. And when
I tell my Loki stories, they say they've heard
them all before. Dad's thin face sags into a scowl
and he picks the wood chippings out of his grey
beard. Mum slumps down next to him, fixes her
small blue eyes down on her embroidery, and
starts to yawn.

I don't care. At least I find my Loki stories
exciting. Loki is the naughtiest of all the gods,
and he loves playing tricks on the others. They

get so annoyed with him that they tie him to a stone under a snake that drips poison onto his face. His wife tries to catch the poison in a bowl, but whenever she goes off to empty the bowl, it goes all over his face and he screams in agony, making the whole world shake.

Anyway, it's spring again now, so I don't have to spend my evenings telling my amazing stories to an ungrateful audience. I can stay outside, playing raiders with Astrid. She brought a shield as well as a sword today, but we weren't able to use it properly because it's new and her dad would notice marks on it.

But it still felt good to grasp it and pretend I was charging into a village of weak locals.

GET REAL

The Vikings worshipped many gods and goddesses, all of whom had distinct personalities. These included Odin, the ruler of the gods and the god of war, Thor, the god of thunder and storms, and Loki, a mischievous shapeshifter.

Fifth Day

Astrid couldn't play at raiding with me today as she was helping her dad Frode with his work. He has blond hair like her, and you can see where she gets her height from. He basically looks like a version of her that's been stretched and roasted over an open fire. He works bare-chested, and his skin is covered in red marks from where the metal has burnt him.

He spends all his time standing next to a huge clay mound with a fire inside that's called a 'furnace'. It's so hot that metal goes soft when you stick it inside. He gets chunks of metal from rocks, or broken weapons, and hammers them into new shapes.

Astrid stands next to him and pushes a huge leather bag called the 'bellows', which keeps the furnace hot. The heat makes it a good place to be in winter, but it's a shame to waste a nice day like today there.

I asked Frode if Astrid could come to the forest with me, and he said they'd both need to work hard as he'd heard that a group of raiders were moving their ship across land towards us.

I panicked and cowered on the floor with my head in my hands. I couldn't stop myself imagining the raiders stealing all my stuff, chopping me into pieces and then setting me on fire for good measure.

Frode laughed and said they weren't coming here to raid. If they were, they'd hardly push their boat overland. They'd surprise us at night, creeping up so stealthily that we'd know nothing about it until our heads had been split into two soggy halves. I think this was meant to be reassuring, but it only made me whimper even louder.

He said he'd met the raiders before. They're led by a huge man with a gruff voice called Ulf. They sometimes cut across the forest to the east of our village rather than follow the river all the way north and sail back down the coast. Frode wasn't making new weapons to fight them, but to trade with them.

My breathing went back to normal and I got up from the floor and wiped the tiny scraps of metal from my tunic.

Sixth Day

I can't believe I got frightened about the raiders yesterday. I shouldn't be worrying about them. In fact, this is my big chance. All I have to do is show them that I'm worthy of joining their crew, and I can set out across the sea for a life of adventure and mayhem.

I could even invite Astrid along for the fun. She was helping her dad again today, so I had to practise fighting on my own. Frode said I could take one of his axes as long as I didn't get scared and run away from it. Ha ha. He'll see how scared of danger I really am when the raiders ask me to join them and I grab lots of amazing treasure.

As well as honing my axe skills, I thought about how to introduce myself to the raiders when they arrive. I considered running out at them with my axe held high to prove how fierce I am, but I realised they'd probably think I was attacking them and slice me in two before I could explain myself.

It's fine. I just need to calmly greet them and explain why I would be a worthy addition to their crew.

Seventh Day

I heard thudding from the forest to the east of our village this morning and raced towards it.

The first thing I saw was a wooden dragon's head emerging on the path between the trees. But rather than gliding smoothly as it would on water, it was juddering from side to side.

Behind it were about forty men with filthy tunics, ripped leggings and boots that were caked in mud. They were running around the bottom of a long and narrow ship that was being dragged along on tree trunks. Some of the men were pulling the ship forward, whilst others were working in pairs to carry the trunks from the back of the ship to the front.

Even though Frode had told me what to expect, it was still very strange to see a ship travelling through a forest. Not as weird as seeing someone riding a horse across the sea would be, but close.

As I approached the group, I could make out a man with straggly ginger hair and a few missing teeth who must have been Ulf, the leader. He was growling instructions to the others as he examined the ship.

I raced up to him and announced that I was
a fearless raider who wanted to join his crew.
Unfortunately, he didn't hear, and kept
shouting at his men.

I tapped him on the shoulder so I could say it
again. It turned out not to be a great idea to
surprise a grizzled old raider. He shoved me to
the muddy floor, drew his sword and pressed it
to my throat. It was so sharp that a single burp
could have killed me. I was glad I hadn't eaten
too much porridge that morning.

I begged him not to kill me, and told him that
he could have anything he wanted if he let me
live, including my collection of carved Thor and
Loki figures.

He nodded, tucked his sword back into its
sheath and asked me what I wanted from him.

24

I told him I was a fearsome warrior and wanted to join his crew.

Looking back, I can see that might not have been the best time to make the announcement.

My knees were still shaking and my voice was broken and squeaky.

He snorted out a laugh and went back to shouting at the others. I tried to explain that I'd been practising and would be brilliant at raiding, but he took no notice.

I realised that actions would speak louder than words. I sprinted around to the back of the ship to pick up the end of a log. I shoved my hands underneath it and tried to hoist it up. Even though I put all of my strength into it, it wouldn't budge.

A man with red hair jogged around from the front and took the other end. Between us, we managed to get it into the air. My arms were quaking from the effort, and I felt like giving up and asking if there were something else I could do to impress them instead.

But I forced myself to stagger on. All I had to do was make it to the front of the ship, drop it to the ground and act like it had been no big deal.

The man with red hair lifted his end of the trunk onto his shoulder. I tried to do the same.

The pain hit me right away. My whole arm ached, my knees buckled and my feet slipped on the muddy ground. The log was going to push me into the ground as if I were a nail. I let go.

The red-haired man yelped with agony as the full weight of the trunk pressed on him. He yelled at me for being an idiot, and one of the others had to come over and grab my end.

Ulf ran back over to me and drew his sword again. This time I wasn't going to be able to talk my way out of it. I turned and ran back to the village.

GET REAL

One of the reasons the Vikings were so successful as traders and raiders was their longships. They were narrow enough to travel down rivers, and light enough to be rolled over the ground on logs. Some believe they had dragons' heads carved at the front to frighten people as they approached.

Eighth Day

The raiders moored their ship in the harbour yesterday morning and spent the rest of the day putting up their tents and trading their plundered goods for weapons, clothes, wheat and dried fish. Our village leader, Birger, has said he's happy for them to stay and share our

food for a while, which is unusually generous for him. I expect it has something to do with the fancy new silver brooch he's been wearing.

Astrid finished her work in the afternoon, so she was free to spend the day spying on the raiders with me. We watched them fill their water buckets from our wells and wash their tunics and leggings in our stream.

In the evening, they sat around the harbour drinking ale and boasting about how many people they'd killed. We couldn't resist approaching them and telling them all about our raiding skills, but they weren't interested.

The red-haired raider, who turned out to be called Arne, was comparing scars with a tall raider with black hair. Arne had a wide diagonal scar across his chest that had been

made by a sword. The tall raider had a long
thin one across his chin that had been made by
a knife. I tried to join in by showing them the
cut I made on my leg with the axe. It wasn't
as big as either of theirs, so I made up a story
about how I'd got it on a raid where I'd stolen
hundreds of rings, brooches and beads.

They were starting to look impressed, but then
a raider with three fingers and one ear missing
came over to show off his war wounds. There
was no way anyone could compete with that.

Luckily, I
haven't lost my
good looks!

Ninth Day

I've found out what the raiders are planning.
A trader has told them about a small village
on the east coast of England, which has lots of
valuable treasure and hardly anyone capable
of defending it. They're going to sail across the
sea, take all the valuable stuff from it and come
back here.

That sounds perfect. I could go with them,
join in with the raid and come right back. The
English village is an easy target, and I'll be
with some very experienced fighters, so I'll be
in no danger. I'll get some excellent raiding
experience and I won't be away long. There's no
way Mum and Dad can object to that.

Later

Dad and Mum have objected. They think it will be too dangerous, even though I've explained that it won't be. I've warned them that I'm going to keep asking until they agree, but they don't think I actually mean it. They'll find out.

33

Tenth Day

My plan was to keep asking all night, but I think I must have fallen asleep whilst speaking. I woke them both up before dawn with the same question. I kept going as Dad ate his bread and buttermilk and Mum brought the fire back to life.

All morning, I went back and forth from inside our house, where Mum was grinding corn to make flour, to the yard opposite, where Dad was carving a long wooden plank. I asked my question over and over again, even though they were pretending that they couldn't hear me.

Finally, Dad snapped. He said the raiders probably wouldn't want me, but he'd ask them if I promised to shut up.

I didn't trust him to explain my skills properly, so I went along with him.

I'm glad I did, because all Dad asked when
he found Ulf was if he wanted to take a
fourteen-year-old boy who couldn't shut up
with them. Obviously, Ulf said no. He also
recognised me from the other day and said
that even if he did, he wouldn't choose one
who'd risk the lives of his crew by dropping
trees on them.

I explained that I only wanted to go on one
raid to see what it was like, and promised
to be very quiet. He scratched his beard
and thought about it for a while. Then he
said he'd gather his men in the centre of the
village tomorrow morning, and set me three
challenges. If I passed them, he'd let me come.

So it's all worked out brilliantly. I'm bound
to pass his tests after all the training I've
done. I'm sure I'll be off raiding with my new
friends very soon.

Chapter 2
Viking trials

Eleventh Day

I found the raiders gathered on the flat strip of land outside Birger's house. I pushed through and found an axe and spear lying on the ground. A few of the raiders were pointing and laughing at me, but I took no notice. I was about to prove them wrong.

Ulf dragged an old wooden barrel, which was full of straw, along the grass. He said he was going to start with an easy one. I had to throw the axe into the side of the barrel.

After all the practice I'd had throwing my axe at trees, this seemed like it would be simple. I stared at the barrel and felt the weight of the axe in my hand.

The raiders stomped their feet, clapped their hands and shouted 'go'. Not only did this break my concentration, but it got the attention of everyone in the village, who joined the crowd to see what was going on.

Men, women and children swarmed around on both sides. Dad and Frode appeared and pushed people back, reminding them that an axe might not necessarily go straight ahead if I am the one throwing it.

I spotted Astrid on my left. She was telling everyone to be quiet, so I could focus. At least someone was being sensible.

Birger emerged from his house and told everyone to get back to work. His long grey hair was flopping about in the wind, and his cracked cheeks were even redder than usual. Ulf explained that I'd been set some special challenges, and everyone wanted to enjoy the entertainment. Birger sighed and said everyone could watch as long as they went back to work straight afterwards.

I tried to block it all out and pretend I was back in the forest with no one but Astrid nearby. I took a deep breath, lifted the axe and let it go.

It spun through the air, the ornamental silver lines on the blade catching the sunlight as it went. It was heading right for the middle of the barrel. It wasn't just going to hit the thing. It was going to smash it to pieces.

But right at the last minute, it curved to the left. It swept so close to the barrel that it could have shaved splinters off it, but it landed helplessly on the grass beyond.

I blamed the wind and begged Ulf to let me have another go. He refused, saying that I only got one attempt at each challenge. I tried to look on the bright side. I hadn't killed anyone yet. And if I did well enough on the next two challenges, he might still accept me.

Ulf dragged the barrel a few feet further back and told me the next challenge would be to hit it with the spear.

I grabbed the weapon and held it up, trying to work out the best place to grip it. Unlike the axe, I hadn't had any practice with one of these.

I breathed slowly in and out, staring at the barrel. All I had to do was aim the spear and release it. It was simple.

I ran forward and let it go. Or at least, I tried to. The weapon didn't fly through the air like I was expecting. It just plummeted down to the grass. I should probably have released it sooner or something. But how was I to know? I'd never even touched one before.

The raiders laughed and shook their heads.

There was still one remaining challenge, and one chance to prove myself.

Ulf approached me with a flaming torch in his hand. He said the last challenge was the hardest of all. I had to throw the flaming torch into the barrel and set the straw on fire. It was a vital skill if you wanted to burn a village.

Then he pulled the barrel back even further.

I grabbed the handle of the torch and felt the heat of the flame. Surely there was no way anyone could throw the torch all that way?

I looked around, wondering if there was something I was missing. Then I had an idea. I stepped forward and picked up the spear again. Then I undid my belt and tied the end of the burning torch to the spear.

I glanced over at Ulf and grinned, as if to tell him I'd worked out his little puzzle. He looked slightly confused, but was probably just reflecting on how useful it would be to have someone so cunning on his crew.

I took three steps back, held my flaming spear in position and ran forward. This time I

released it sooner, and it flew up into the air.
I watched it go, waiting for the moment that
the spear would arc down and hit the barrel. It
didn't come.

The spear kept on soaring higher, and passed
straight over the top of the barrel.

I sighed. I'd missed the target for the third
time. I'd failed all my tasks.

That turned out to be the least of my worries.
There were gasps and shrieks from the crowd,
and at first I couldn't work out what was going
on. Then I saw. The burning spear was heading
right towards the straw roof of Birger's house.
I found myself running towards it, as if I could
catch up with it and stop it. But the spear hit the
roof, and bright orange flames spread across it.

Birger ran to his house, and the crowd followed. A few people who lived nearby grabbed water barrels from their houses and yelled at the swarming crowd to let them through. Others scrabbled around the well, frantically pulling at the rope to get the bucket. Some grabbed cups and bowls and ran back and forth from the stream to Birger's house, desperate to make whatever difference they could.

Eventually, they got the fire out. The straw had completely burned away, leaving just the charred wooden frame underneath. Birger angrily announced that the entire roof would have to be rebuilt.

Dad offered to make me do it, but Birger said he needed skilled craftsmen, not useless children. Then Dad told him that I'd personally pay for the damage by working in the shipyard every day for a year without a break.

Why did he have to say that? Birger wasn't asking me to do anything, except stay away from him. Now I've got a whole year of boredom ahead of me when I should be out raiding.

Twelfth Day

Dad woke me before the cock had crowed and told me to get to work. He said I wasn't allowed any food until he was satisfied with what I'd done.

He marched me to his end of the yard, handed me an adze, and told me to shape a plank of wood into a steering oar, with a handle and a wide, rounded end.

I tapped away at the wood, muttering to myself. I couldn't face a whole year of this, just because of one tiny mistake. If anything, the raiders should have been impressed by my burning skills and begged me to join them.

An idea came to me. It was brilliant and simple. I could still join the raiders if I wanted to, just without their permission. If I sneaked onto their boat, hid under some animal skins and didn't reveal myself until we were out at sea, they'd have no choice but to let me join them.

They'd probably admire my commitment so much that they'd realise they should have accepted me in the first place. And when I got back, I'd be carrying so much treasure that Mum and Dad would forgive me right away.

As I was thinking about my plan, I realised that I'd shaved too much wood away from one side of the plank. I tried evening it out on the other side, but I ended up with something that was more like a handle than a steering oar. I hid it under a pile of wood and started on another one.

Dad eventually emerged and said I could take a break for some bread and cheese. I told him I'd rather keep on going with my work, and he nodded and went back inside. When I was sure he couldn't see, I raced over to Astrid's house and told her about what I'm going to do.

She said it was a brilliant idea, and she wanted to come too. I made it clear that raiding was very dangerous and we'd almost certainly lose at least one limb each, but she insisted. I was secretly glad about this.

She has promised to bring shields and axes from her dad's workshop, and meet me next to the raider's ship in the middle of the night. Whilst they're sleeping, we're going to sneak on board, hide and stay perfectly still until we're far out to sea.

I rushed back to my plank and adze just in time to see Dad coming out of our house. I couldn't stop myself grinning, and he looked very suspicious. Tomorrow he'll know exactly why I was smiling, but by then it will be too late.

Chapter 3
Stowaways

Thirteenth Day

I stayed awake long after Dad and Mum were snoring last night. It wasn't hard to stop myself from sleeping, as I was so excited about my coming adventure. I stuffed my fox skins, parchments and quill into a cloth sack and tiptoed out.

Astrid was already at the harbour when I arrived, with the stuff she'd grabbed from her dad's workshop. She handed me an axe that was decorated with swirly silver lines, and a shield made of light wood that had been painted red. It had a metal boss on the front and a grip on the back. I asked Astrid if she felt bad about taking them, and she said her dad would be able to afford a hundred more with the plunder we'll get. Good point.

The raiders were asleep in their tents, so we clambered onto their ship. The space inside was long and narrow, with rows of wooden storage chests placed next to the oarholes. There was a tangled mess of cloth sacks, animal skins, woollen blankets and rope around the mast, which seemed like the best place to hide.

We scooped the pile aside, releasing the stench of stale seawater, and burrowed in. I placed my shield on top of my chest, then covered myself with sacks.

I thought I would be too frightened of being discovered to fall asleep, but the next thing I knew it was light, and footsteps were thudding all around me.

The raiders were back on the ship, and were preparing to set off. The pile on top of me grew heavier as tents were thrown onto it. I felt a heavy boot stomping over my chest, and was glad of the shield.

I heard Astrid letting out a quiet cry, and I guessed the same thing had happened to her.

After what seemed like a lifetime of grunting

and shouting, I heard the splash of oars hitting the water and felt us moving.

I wondered how long I should leave it before jumping out. If I did it too soon, they'd just throw me overboard and tell me to swim back. But I didn't think I could stand lying under all that smelly stuff forever.

About an hour later, the decision was made for me. I heard Arne shouting that the ropes were moving and there could be something underneath them. I couldn't risk him jabbing his sword in to stab a stowaway fox or hare, so I had no choice but to rise up and announce that I'd come along to help them.

The raiders were arranged in rows down both sides of the ship, sitting on the storage chests and pushing their oars in time. They all stopped to look.

Ulf strode towards me without saying a word, grabbed me under the shoulders and told Arne to get my feet. Then they swung me back and forth, building up enough momentum to make sure I'd be well away from the boat when I splashed into the sea. I tried to gabble out an explanation about how useful I could be, but they took no notice.

It was only when Astrid jumped out that they stopped and put me down.

She said she was sorry we'd sneaked on, but we just wanted to help with the raid. Ulf pointed at me and said I'd be about as useful as a glass shield. I was hoping Astrid would leap to my defence, but she asked if it really mattered anyway. If we were so terrible, we'd simply get killed right away, which is the same thing that would happen if they threw us overboard.

Ulf said he'd think about it. Then said we should sit at the back of the boat and stay completely silent, and told the others to get back to their rowing.

Fourteenth Day

I imagined the raiders would be out on the open sea by now, but in fact they don't go too far from the shore. I can see it passing on our left as we travel south. Every night the raiders pull the ship onto a beach, pitch their tents and search the land for berries and fresh water.

I'm too scared to talk to Ulf, but Arne is happy enough to answer my questions. He's explained that if they sail down the coast, they'll eventually get to a narrow stretch of sea that

will take them across to England. The village
the trader tipped them off about is a day's sail
north from the crossing.

I asked why they don't just stop wherever they
want and take what they want, but he said a
raid needs careful planning. It's much better
to bribe traders and travellers to find out if
they've seen anywhere that would be good to
raid than wade into a battle that they might
lose. There are plenty of defenceless villages
and weak monks sitting on huge piles of silver
if you know where to find them.

GET REAL

*The Viking Age is said to have begun in
793 AD with the raid on the monastery
on the island of Lindisfarne. The Vikings
killed monks, stole precious crosses and
cups and set fire to buildings.*

Fifteenth Day

Ulf has said we're not allowed to eat any of the supplies of dried fish, but Arne has been kind enough to give us some of his share, and Astrid is good at finding berries when we're on shore, so we haven't gone hungry.

It's just as well, because we'll need our strength when we attack the village. I'm actually quite disappointed it's going to be so defenceless. I'd have liked a challenge.

We've been sleeping under our animal skins on the deck every night, as there aren't any spare tents for us. But even though it's been cold, it hasn't been wet, and we're both getting plenty of rest.

Ulf hasn't actually said he's letting us join the raid yet, but I'm sure he would have thrown us overboard by now if he wasn't going to.

Sixteenth Day

One of the raiders, who is called Njal, was very ill today after eating some dodgy berries last night. He had to leave his oar so he could lean over the back of the ship and throw up.

Spotting a chance to prove how useful I could be, I sat down on his storage chest and took over. The other rowers were all moving in perfect time, and I tried to go along with them. But I kept finding that my oar clacked into the one in front or behind. I managed to get it into the water a few times, but it really hurt

my arms to push it through and pull it back up again. I was amazed they had the strength to do this all day.

Eventually, my flailing disrupted the others, and everyone on my side came to a stop, which meant we began to turn.

Ulf stepped over to see what was going on, and yelled at me to return to the back.

Astrid took over, and kept going all day without any problems. But I think the wind must have picked up and made it easier for her.

It was quite boring sitting at the back without her. I had to settle for telling my Loki stories to Njal, but the sick was pretty much coming out of his ears by then, so I don't think that he could hear me.

Seventeenth Day

We are now crossing the open sea. I asked Ulf if he'd decided whether we could join the raid or not. Sadly, he said he wanted us to wait behind and guard the ship. As if our ship would need defending against a bunch of pathetic villagers who couldn't even lift an axe, let alone plant one in a skull.

I said we'd only joined him to see what a raid was like, and the least he could do was let us watch, but he wouldn't budge. He said that a successful raid relies on terror. In many cases, the villagers are so petrified they simply hand over their valuables without the need for a battle. A couple of kids tagging along will make them look more like a family outing than a pack of ravening wolves.

He's probably just worried that we'll be better at raiding than him, and get to all the good stuff first.

It doesn't matter anyway. Astrid and I have come up with a plan. We'll agree to protect the ship, but when the others set off, we'll follow behind and join in. They'll be so busy fighting, they probably won't even notice that we're fighting too.

So that settles it. I'm finally about to go raiding. I'll be rich beyond my wildest dreams and covered in glory by the next time I write on this piece of parchment.

Eighteenth Day

It was dark when we reached the stretch
of coast the trader had described. It was a
sheltered bay overlooked by a small, steep hill
with a circle of trees on top.

There was a wide river snaking off at the far
side. The village was ten minutes along it on
foot, in the middle of a dark patch of trees.

The raiders shoved the boat onto the sand, and
put their armour on. Some of them had helmets
with metal circles to protect their eyes, some
had chain mail vests and some had shields with
bright patterns of yellow, red and green. They
lined up along the beach, holding their axes
and spears, and shouting to get themselves into
the mood for violence.

It's easy to see why villagers would whimper with

fright and hand over their valuables. They looked like a wall made of wood, metal and beards.

The first pink streaks of morning were appearing in the east when Ulf gave the order to advance. They marched away down the sandy bank next to the stream whilst we remained in front of the ship, holding up our axes and shields as if ready to defend it.

As we watched them go, I asked Astrid when she thought we should abandon our post and follow them. Too soon, and Ulf might spot us. Too late and we could miss all the fun. She told me to hold on until they had reached the edge of the forest.

As soon as they did, we began to run. It was hard to go fast whilst carrying the shield and axe. I don't know how the others managed with all that armour.

Astrid's weapons must have been lighter because she got quite far ahead of me, and I had to hiss at her to wait.

Yellow light was spreading across the sky as we approached the wood, but everything went dark again when we dashed into it.

I caught up with Astrid behind a large oak tree. She said we should wait until we heard something from the village before going on. The last thing we wanted to do was to spoil a surprise attack.

I stood next to her and got my breath back. I could hear the river running next to us, the waves breaking behind us and lots of birds chirping above us, but nothing at all ahead. Maybe the villagers were handing over their stuff in total silence.

A few moments later, it started. There were deep roars and stomping feet, followed by terrified screams.

The sounds were still faint, though. We hadn't quite reached the village yet.

We ran on. As I went, I felt like the noises were changing. The roaring of the raiders had been replaced by grunting and clanking metal. The locals had obviously decided to put up some sort of fight after all.

I found myself slowing down. This was it. This was the fight I'd been waiting for my whole life. And now I could join in. So why did I want to turn back?

Astrid sprinted into the dark trees and was gone. That settled it. I could hardly go back to the boat whilst she was fighting. I'd never hear the last of it.

I crept forward until I reached the edge of the clearing where the village had been built. I could see frantic blurs of movement in the weak morning light. A fierce battle was going on.

I could see the huge, hulking outlines of the raiders, swinging their axes and raising their shields. But they were struggling against others who were just as big and strong. The trader had given them false information. This wasn't just a village full of old people and children. There were plenty of capable adults here, maybe enough to outnumber us.

The villagers had been surprised by the attack, and were fighting in their leggings and tunics instead of armour. But they'd managed to grab their weapons. I saw a man from the village slash at one of our raiders with a sword. The raider raised his shield and blocked it, but a woman from the village swept round and stabbed him in the side with her knife. He fell down, screaming and clutching his side.

I suddenly realised what an important job I'd been given by Ulf. Guarding the ship was a great responsibility, and I should return to it right away.

I was about to head back when I spotted
something. A large figure was leaning over a
smaller one and drawing back his sword. As the
gloomy shapes became clearer, I could see that
a man with straggly black hair was looming
over Astrid, who was flailing around in the mud.

I surprised myself by running towards them.
I found myself raising my axe above my head,
and heading straight for the villager.

I did my best to let out a vicious battle cry, but
all that came out was a weird high noise. At
least it distracted the villager, who turned to look
at me, giving Astrid the chance to scrabble away.

He gave up on her and decided to point his
sword at me instead.

I kept running, unsure what to do next. It
occurred to me that if I kept on going, I'd end

74

up impaling myself on his sword without him having to do any work at all. It would hardly be a heroic death.

I remembered I was holding an axe, and decided to throw it at him. I swung it in the air and let go. Somehow it managed to land behind me. Next, I tried to throw my shield, but it just sank into the mud.

The man looked at me in confusion, probably wondering what sort of battle tactic throwing away your weapons could be.

Then something very strange happened. He screamed, and coughed up blood. I wondered if my axe had somehow bounced off a tree and managed to hit him after all.

But then I saw Arne behind him, grasping his axe, which was dripping deep red blood.

The villager staggered around. Arne had cut a huge gash into his back, and dark blood was spreading down the lower half of his tunic.

Arne yelled at me to run, but I couldn't stop myself gazing around at the madness I was in the middle of.

So this was a raid. I'd always imagined they would be glorious and heroic, but this was just dirty and desperate. In the growing light, I could see people swinging axes, lifting shields and falling to the slippery ground. They were grunting, wincing and crying. Sweat and blood and vomit were drenching armour and clothing, and the smell was unbearable.

Someone yanked my arm. I saw that Astrid was beside me. She put her axe down, slapped me on the cheek and said we needed to get back to the ship.

I managed to take my eyes off the carnage, and we made for the forest. Just as we were getting to it, Astrid pointed at a small hut to our left and said we should take the chance to plunder something from it.

I didn't fancy going inside without my axe. Even a small child armed with a wooden toy boat would be able to fend me off. But before I could say anything, Astrid ran in with her muddy shield pressed to her chest and her axe raised. A moment later, she stuck her head around the door and told me that there was no one there.

There were only a few weak embers in the hearth, and dim light from the door. I grabbed some objects on the floor and went outside to see what I'd got. I'd managed to plunder a comb, two spoons and a toothpick. It wasn't exactly the greatest treasure haul ever.

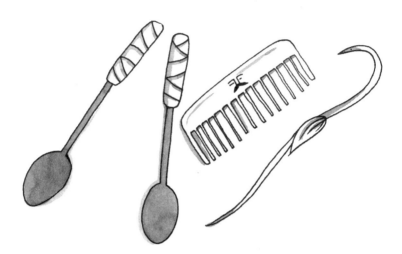

Astrid rushed out carrying a small leather bag. She opened it to show that there were dozens of silver coins inside. She said I could share it if I liked. I dropped my disappointing items and we headed back into the forest.

As we neared the other side, I could make out a red flickering in the distance, and I wondered if we'd gone the wrong way, and were about to emerge into a different village. But as we cleared the trees, I could see the flames were coming from the beach.

Our ship was burning. Two men with torches were on board, setting light to the mast and oars. Another was leaning over to the dragon head, and trying to get that going too.

We stopped at the edge of the trees and stared at the longboat. We had been given one job, which was to protect the ship. We'd left it, and now it had been destroyed. Even if the raiders somehow defeated the villagers and made it back in time to save their ship, we wouldn't be welcome on it ever again.

So what could we do? We couldn't run back to the gruesome battle, and we couldn't go to the ship. We had no choice but to head inland.

We trudged over a wide, flat plain and into another forest.

By the time we emerged from it, light rain was falling and a cold wind was blowing. Astrid used her shield to protect herself from the drizzle, but I just had to untie my belt and lift my tunic over my head.

We kept on walking all day, plodding along soggy land with no idea where we were going.

This isn't the kind of adventure I had in mind.

Now Astrid has made a shelter from her shield and some branches against the side of a tree, so we can at least stay dry until morning.

I hope they don't have dragons around here.

Nineteenth Day

I have decided that I don't want to be a raider after all. It wasn't as much fun as I expected.

Dad was right. I should have stayed at home and learned how to make ships. I suppose I'll have to go back and admit that now, though I've no idea how I'm going to. We don't even know which way to walk.

Astrid found some berries this evening, and we stumbled across a stream we could drink from. I need more rest now. Maybe we'll work out what to do in the morning.

Chapter 4

⊢─┤

Hitching a ride

Twentieth Day

Astrid pointed out that if we want to get back home, we'll have to cross the sea, which means heading back to the coast.

It might seem obvious, but we were in a state of confusion yesterday, and it was hard for us to think straight.

If we go back the way that we came, we'll both get killed by the villagers. So we need to find a new stretch of coast and work out what to do from there.

The problem was that we both thought we had to walk in opposite directions to get there. Astrid insisted on going her way, so I struck out on my own. But then I remembered she had the shield and axe, so I'd better follow her.

As it turned out, we did eventually come to the sea. But I expect the coastline curves around, so we were both right.

We are now on a rocky beach looking out at the choppy waves. I wonder how wide this stretch of sea is? Maybe we could swim across.

Twenty—First Day

We spent a rough night on the lumpy pebbles at the top of the beach. Rain woke us just after dawn and we spent a few hours gazing out at the ocean through light mist.

I spotted something through the haze. A small shape was bobbing about. I ran towards the crashing waves to get a closer look. I longed to see the wooden face of a dragon gliding toward us. A sight that was meant to inspire terror would have brought me great comfort. But it was a small cargo ship, with no scary beast on the front.

Astrid waded into the sea and waved her arms around. I told her to be careful. If they were local sailors, they wouldn't be happy when they found out how we got here. Astrid said we could talk our way round it.

The gusty air blew into my face as I plodded after her. The cold sea splashed over my leggings and tunic, and I had to hold my shivering arms over my chest.

A figure at the front of the ship pointed to us. The sails were pulled up, and oars appeared over the sides. They steered the ship towards us, and we waded further in.

An oar splashed into the water next to Astrid. She grabbed it, the man pulled her up and she scrambled onto the deck. The oar returned to the water near where I was. I tried to grab it, but the wood was too slippery and I couldn't get a grip. A wave crashed over me, filling my mouth and nostrils with saltwater.

I tried again, and this time I managed to get just far enough up for the man to grab my tunic and haul me in.

I collapsed to the floor, spitting out seawater and trying to convince him that we weren't raiders. I don't think anyone was listening, though, as Astrid struck up a conversation with the man before I'd finished.

I could tell from his voice that he was from our land, so there was no need to invent excuses for why we were there. Astrid admitted that we'd sneaked along on a raid, it hadn't gone well and now we needed to head back.

The man, who was called Skarde, said he could take us back home eventually, but he had another stop to make first. It all depended how much we could pay him.

Astrid produced four silver coins from her bag, said that they were all we had and that he could take them or leave them.

I tried to point out that we actually had plenty more coins if he wanted those too, but Astrid pressed her soaking foot down over my mouth. Then I realised that Astrid was lying so we could save some of the coins for when we were home, which was very smart.

Skarde agreed to take us for four coins. He warned us that we wouldn't be going the most direct way, and I said it was fine. We'd been rescued from a strange, flat land and now we

were heading home. Why should I care which route we took?

Twenty–Second Day

Skarde is carrying several huge bundles of wool to a place called 'Iceland'. This sounds like it will be very cold, and I wish I hadn't left my animal skins on the other ship. Skarde has said we can lie under the wool bundles if we want to keep warm, as long as we don't unwrap any of them or get them dirty.

I told Astrid to offer him one of her remaining coins for a bundle of wool so we could use it as a blanket, but she said we'd have to admit we had more coins after all, and there would be nothing to stop him from taking the rest.

I suppose she's right. But we might want to swap all our remaining coins for something warm by the time we reach the land of ice.

Twenty–Third Day

We are heading north along the coast, and Skarde says we're making good progress. Our journey on this ship has been very different from the last one. There are only fourteen people on board, including us. And they use the sail to travel, rather than rowing, except for when they need to get to the shore and back.

It's much quieter, with more silent staring at the sea and less shouting and grunting. At night, they find a sheltered spot to anchor the ship, but rather than going on land and setting up tents, they sleep under skins and blankets.

We are still eating dried fish, but at least we're getting a better share this time. I suppose that's what you get for paying your way.

Twenty⸺Fourth Day

Today we sailed past the last of the coast and over the sea to an island. Skarde and the others rowed us to the shore and we jumped down onto the beach. Ahead of us was a grassy slope leading up to a small cluster of huts, and I mentioned to Skarde that Iceland wasn't as cold as I was expecting. In fact, it didn't look too different from the land we'd just sailed past.

Skarde laughed. He said we weren't in Iceland yet. This was merely our last stop before we set out on our main voyage across the open sea. He said they were off to trade some of the wool with the locals for food, so we should enjoy our last hours on land for a few days.

A few days? How far away is this Iceland place, exactly?

GET REAL

Orkney is a group of islands to the north-east of mainland Scotland. Viking travellers settled there, and on nearby Shetland, in the 8th and 9th centuries. They became important bases for trade, and launching points for raids.

Twenty—Fifth Day

We're out on the open sea again, with no land in sight. Sometimes the wind blows us along, and it feels like we're going somewhere. At other times, it dies down, and I remember I'm floating in the middle of the ocean on a few overlapping pieces of wood when I could have stayed at home in my comfortable bed next to a warm hearth.

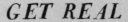
GET REAL

Viking ships were built from overlapping planks, which is known as 'clinker' construction. The planks were fastened together with nails, and gaps were filled with wool and animal hair to make the vessels watertight.

Twenty—Sixth Day

I tried telling my Loki stories to Skarde today. He said the stories were very good, but he was too busy to hear them. The thing he was busy with was staring at the sea and occasionally giving instructions to his crew, so his excuse wasn't very convincing. But he handed me a bag of dice carved from bone, and told me to play with those.

For the rest of the day, Astrid and I rolled the dice to see who could get the highest score. It made the time go surprisingly fast, especially as we kept making up new imaginary prizes for the winner, like a whole pot of meat stew, a huge pile of bear skins and a magical hearth that you could light in the middle of a ship without burning it down.

Twenty-Seventh Day

The sea was rough today, and we couldn't even play dice because they kept rolling all over the boat and getting under everyone's feet. I had nothing to do except tell my Loki stories to Astrid. Even she asked if I could stop, so I had to mutter them to myself instead.

Our small ship is bobbing frantically up and down, and my stomach is turning with every violent drop. I can't even continue with this because my handwriting is so wobbly I'll never be able to read it back.

Twenty-Eighth Day

The sea is calmer, but the wind is very bitter now, and the rest of the crew are huddling under their thick animal skins. I tried doing star jumps on one of the benches to keep warm, but I overbalanced and almost knocked one of the crew into the sea. Now I've been ordered to sit still until we arrive.

Chapter 5

⟞

A land of ice?

Twenty—Ninth Day

Greetings from Iceland! We are finally here.
Despite the name, it isn't really made of ice.
So far, I can see black beaches and sharp
rocks that jut out of the sea like the claws of a
drowned monster. I have no idea why anyone
would choose to build a new settlement on a
land like this. It looks like somewhere Thor
vented his anger on after a particularly bad
argument with his dad.

It turns out that Iceland is a huge island, and
the settlement we're heading for is on the west
side, so we won't even get there until tomorrow.
At least when I get there, I'll know it's as far
west as I'll ever go and that it will be time to
head back.

GET REAL

The Viking world expanded in the ninth and tenth centuries, and Iceland was settled as a colony from around 874 AD. Many Norwegians moved there, drawn by the chance to set up farms. The island was named Iceland by an explorer called Flóki Vilgerðarson, who discovered a fjord blocked by ice.

First Day of the New Moon

This morning we sailed around a huge spike of land that jutted far out into the sea, and moored our ship in a wide, sheltered bay. We finally arrived at the village, more than a week after Skarde told us he had to make a stop on the way home. He wasn't lying when he said it wasn't a direct route.

The town that stretched along the bay consisted of long houses with stone bases, wooden frames with walls of turf and roofs covered in grass. Skarde pointed to one and said that we could sleep in it tonight. It will be a luxury to have actual shelter over our heads after all those nights of cowering under the wool.

Tomorrow, Skarde is going to trade the wool for some new cargo to take home with us. I hope it's something comfortable. I don't want to spend the journey back trying to keep myself warm under a pile of glass jars or broken metal scraps.

The locals are about to serve us a mutton stew now, and it will be the first hot food that I've had in weeks.

Second Day

I've found out what the cargo for the way back is going to be. And it's even worse than I could have imagined.

Skarde and his men spent the morning unloading the wool and haggling with the locals. When they moved back towards the ship, I noticed that some of them were herding goats.

I asked Skarde what was going on, and he said he'd hoped to get something better from the locals, but the goats would have to do. I asked him where the goats would be travelling, and he said they'd be in the middle of the boat with us.

I made it clear that spending a week next to a goat would be totally unacceptable, and it wasn't the deal he'd offered us. He shrugged and told us we could stay here and wait for the next ship if we wanted to.

Another of the crew said he didn't know what I was complaining about. If I made friends with the goats, they'd let me sleep next to them at night, which would keep me much warmer than a blanket. And if they happened to wee on me, that would be pretty warm too at first.

He laughed and wandered off to get more of the smelly creatures.

Third Day

Skarde and his crew were meant to be setting off this morning, and I was preparing myself for a week of sleeping in goat dung. But something happened that changed our plans entirely.

A ship that looked like Skarde's sailed into the bay. A huge man with long blonde hair and a thick beard jumped out, and twenty others followed him.

At first I thought he was a raider, but no one seemed scared. In fact, they seemed fascinated. They streamed out of their houses and clustered around him.

Skarde told me that the man was Leif Erikson, the son of Erik the Red, who founded the colony in Greenland after he was exiled from here. I hadn't heard of either man, or even the place, but I followed the crowd and beckoned Astrid to come too.

One of Leif's men brought him a wooden chest and he leapt onto it and faced the crowd. In a booming voice, he announced that he had good news to share. I was hoping that he'd discovered a land of self-cooking sheep, but it turned out to be very confusing.

He told us about a man called Jesus from a long

time ago. He died, but then came back to life again, because he was the son of a god.

After he'd finished, the crowd yelled questions at him, and he tackled them one by one.

I told Astrid that Jesus would probably get on well with Thor, as they both had fathers who were gods. But she said I hadn't understood. Leif wasn't telling us about a new god who would sit alongside all the ones we knew. He was saying there was only one god, and all the others weren't real.

I felt myself panicking as I thought this through. If everyone stopped believing in the other gods, no one would want to hear my Loki stories anymore.

The crowd were just as concerned as me, and were yelling their objections, though Leif's normal speaking voice was loud enough to drown them all out.

Astrid ran to the front of the crowd and told them that Leif was right, and they should all listen to him.

Leif grabbed her waist and lifted her up. He said that Astrid had shown great wisdom and they could all learn from her.

Afterwards, I asked her why she'd spoken up, and she said she'd felt sorry for Leif because everyone was shouting at him. He seems like a good friend to have, anyway. His men roasted a pig for him tonight, and he came over and gave us a whole leg to share.

GET REAL

Leif Erikson was an explorer who lived from around 970 AD to 1020 AD. He converted to Christianity in Norway around 999 AD, and set out on a mission to convert other parts of the Viking world to the faith.

Fourth Day

Leif is so pleased that Astrid spoke up for him that he's invited her to join his crew. She's agreed, but only if he lets me come along too, and promises to get us back home. Leif said he'd be glad to, but first he needs to make a quick visit to Greenland so he can tell them about Jesus too.

I told Astrid she could go on her own. I said I'd already gone far enough out of my way, and I just wanted to get home to bed and forget any of this had happened. But then I remembered the filthy goats on Skarde's boat, and decided that anything was better than that.

So it looks like I was wrong after all when I said Iceland was the furthest west I would ever go.

Skarde set off this afternoon. I told him we were cancelling our return journey and asked if we could have one of the coins back, but he refused. It was worth a try, I suppose. I watched them row out to sea and steer around the jagged point of land.

We can't change our minds now. We're sailing with Leif, and home will be even further away. Still, Greenland sounds nice. It's got to be warmer than Iceland with a name like that.

Fifth Day

We are back out at sea again. Astrid offered to give Leif two of her coins for letting us sail with him, but he said all he wanted was for us to pledge our loyalty to him. No one else had ever asked for it, so it was easy to agree.

In exchange, we got plenty of herring, a bear skin each, and we got to keep our coins. A good deal, I reckon.

Sixth Day

I've spent more of my life at sea than on land recently, and this constant violent swaying seems more natural than stillness now.

Leif is always happy to talk, unlike Skarde, but it's hard to get a word in. He's sailed everywhere, and met lots of interesting people, and every story he tells reminds him of another one.

He used to work as a bodyguard for the King of Norway, who converted him to Christianity. Now he's promised to go back to Greenland and get his dad to accept the religion too.

I told him this sounded a little more complicated than the quick stop he'd promised, but he said it would be fine. He was sure his dad would see the light if he explained it properly.

Leif is very forceful, but asking someone to give up all the gods they've ever known in favour of just one is a pretty major change. We could be stuck in Greenland for years.

Seventh Day

The wind was fierce today, but it didn't seem too bad when I wrapped myself in my bearskin.

We're heading north west, towards the very corner of the world. It sounds like a strange place to find a land of lush greenery, but it could be permanently warm up there for all I know.

Eighth Day

We are now sailing around the southern tip of Greenland, and I haven't seen much green so far. I've seen distant snow-capped mountains and a harsh, broken coastline of dark rocks.

It doesn't look like somewhere you would want to go and live. Nothing could grow on the ground, and in winter, the snow would surely cover the whole island.

If anything, this place should be called Iceland, and the one we've just left should be called Greenland instead.

I asked Leif why it's called Greenland, and he said there are a few grassy hills on the other side, but mostly his dad just gave it the name because he was setting up a new colony and wanted to make it sound appealing.

A cunning idea, but I don't think he'll get away with it again. If he calls his next settlement Free-Ale-And-Feasts-Land, no one will believe him.

GET REAL

Erik the Red travelled to Greenland around 982 AD. He spent three years exploring the land and searching for habitable areas. He returned to Iceland, and persuaded the locals to start a new settlement with him. He used the name 'Greenland' to make it sound like an attractive place to live.

Ninth Day

We arrived at the colony this morning, and I have to admit that Leif's dad found a much more pleasant stretch of land than the ragged one we just sailed around. There are some steep stretches of grass around a fjord, so it is quite green after all, though the stark grey mountains in the distance remind you where you really are.

They've managed to build a few of those long huts with the turf walls, and a shaft of sunlight spread across them as we arrived, making the whole place feel surprisingly welcoming.

Leif's dad ran down one of the slopes as he saw us mooring our ship and clambered over the

slimy, dark stones of the beach. He had long red hair and a matching bushy beard, and I could see why he was called Erik the Red.

He boomed questions at us in a voice that was as loud as his son's. I'm surprised Leif even needed to cross the sea to have a conversation with him.

We climbed up the hillside to a wide house with a wooden door, where a crowd had gathered. Leif introduced me to his brothers, Thorvald and Thorstein, who had red hair like their father, and his sister Freydis, who had blonde hair like Leif. They were all as tall and strong as Leif, and had similar powerful voices.

When Leif announced that Astrid and I had pledged our loyalty to him, Freydis congratulated me and slapped me on the back. The force knocked me over and sent me tumbling down the hill.

Tenth Day

We spotted Leif pacing up and down the
hill this morning with a look of intense
concentration. He was being unusually quiet, so
we went over to ask him if anything was wrong.

He said that tomorrow was the day he was
going to gather everyone and tell them about
Christianity. The King of Norway had been
especially keen for him to convert his father
and the rest of his family, so today would be his
big test.

Astrid told him not to worry, because he was
great at speaking, and he'd convinced both of
us about his religion instantly. This seemed to
help him, and he gave us both a firm slap on
the back. I managed to stay upright this time.

After he'd gone, I asked Astrid if she really meant it. I'm not sure I have changed over to Leif's religion yet. So much is happening, I haven't really thought about it. But when I imagine what's beyond our realm, I still think of the burning rainbow linking our world to the halls of Thor, Odin and the rest.

Astrid said she wasn't sure either, but she wanted to make Leif feel better, and that we need all the friends we can get whilst we are stranded on the edge of the world.

Let's just hope that Leif does a great job of converting everyone tomorrow, and he keeps his word and takes us back home soon after.

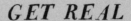

GET REAL

The Vikings believed that the world where humans lived was called Midgard, and that it was linked to Asgard, the land of the gods, by a rainbow bridge called Bifrost.

Eleventh Day

Leif's speech didn't go well. He stood on a wide rock halfway up the hill and got everyone to gather beneath him. He'd barely got started when his dad bellowed out his first objection. Leif tried to explain things calmly, as he'd done in Iceland, but I noticed his hands were shaking slightly this time.

As soon as he got to the bit about there only being one god, Erik flew into a rage and his face went as red as the hair that surrounded it.

He said that he wasn't going to be told what to believe by anyone, especially his own son.

Soon others joined in, and everyone seemed to be yelling at each other. Arguments about borrowed tools and unpaid debts broke out, and Leif couldn't get the topic back round to Christianity.

As if summoned by the commotion, dark clouds swept in, and heavy rain began to pour. Thunder cracked overhead, although most people probably couldn't hear it over the noise of their arguments.

Greenland looked much bleaker with cold rain lashing down. I told myself to get used to it. I had a feeling this matter wouldn't be settled for a very long time.

Twelfth Day

I didn't hear Leif and his dad yelling at each other, so I thought he might have given the missionary work a rest today. But what he was actually doing was explaining it all to his mum, Thjodhild. He had much more success convincing her, and not only does she want to become a Christian, she wants to build a church. Hopefully, she'll get Erik on board, and we can go back home soon.

Thirteenth Day

Or maybe not. Leif converting his mum has only made things worse. Erik announced he was no longer speaking to either of them, then rode his horse over the hill, cursing at the sky.

He's still out now, even though darkness has fallen, and the rest of us are huddled around the hearth in Leif's longhouse.

Fourteenth Day

A ship sailed into the fjord today and a bunch of men with straggly hair and pale, thin faces climbed out and collapsed onto the ground. They were helped up to the houses and given food and drink until they got their strength back.

The leader was called Bjarni, and he was returning here from Iceland to see his parents. Apparently, he had been blown off course, and saw a strange land far to the west.

He managed to get his crew back here by following the stars, though they had to go without food or water for the last four days.

Everyone has been talking about his accidental adventure, and most agree that he imagined it due to spending too long at sea. Apparently, the world comes to an end to the west of here, and if you go any further, you'll bump into a massive sea serpent called Jörmungandr.

I'm sure Bjarni and his crew would have remembered that. They probably just went round and round in circles for a while.

Leif is fascinated by Bjarni's tale and is still questioning him about it now. I'm on the other side of the longhouse from them so I can only hear Leif's loud questions and not Bjarni's quiet replies. He wants to know all about the land Bjarni saw, so he obviously isn't dismissing the story as a fantasy.

Fifteenth Day

Early this morning, Leif told us we'd be setting sail again shortly. A wave of relief swept over me as I realised I'd be away from all these weird places and back home soon.

I questioned him about it, but he said he'd share the good news at a meeting on the hill after everyone had eaten. This should have made me suspicious. Every time he's called a meeting so far, it has ended in disaster.

Leif gathered everyone in front of the flat stone. This time he pulled Astrid and me up onto it too. I smiled and waved at the crowd, trying to hide my terror that Leif might be about to ask me to make a speech about his religion and I wouldn't be able to remember the details.

He began by pointing to Bjarni and reminding everyone of his strange adventure. Bjarni grinned, no doubt happy that at least someone believed his story.

Leif then announced that this new land hadn't been revealed to Bjarni by accident. It was a sign that it was time to form another colony.

He pointed to Astrid and me and announced that the three of us were setting sail in a few days to explore the new land. I tried to keep my smile fixed, but I expect everyone could see the terror in my eyes. My pulse sped up, and I could feel sweat dripping down the back of my tunic, even though it was a cool, grey day.

Leif said he needed to put a crew together, and asked who was with him. There was no reply. I looked out across the weather-beaten faces of the crowd. Most of them were looking down at their boots, or discovering interesting things in their beards that they wanted to examine.

I wondered if now would be a good time to admit that I didn't want to go.

A short man with a brown beard asked if we'd meet Jörmungandr if we sailed too far.

Leif laughed and said that all that stuff about sea monsters circling Midgard was part of the old religion, and God would guide us to a new world of luscious meadows, plentiful fruit and pigs that were slower and more delicious than any found before.

A few of the crew who had travelled with us from Iceland pledged themselves to the journey. It was a shame, because it meant it would definitely happen, but at least it wouldn't just be the three of us sailing to the edge of the world.

Leif kept describing the lush, warm world across the sea, even though the only thing Bjarni had actually told us was that there were trees and mountains.

By the end of his speech, twenty of the locals had agreed to come. So now we have a crew, and we have a ship. If only we had a destination that actually existed, we'd have all the ingredients for a good voyage.

GET REAL

In Viking mythology, Jörmungandr was a sea monster that circled the world of humans with its tail in its mouth. The figure of a serpent or dragon eating its own tail is known as 'ouroboros' and appears in many cultures.

Sixteenth Day

I confessed to Astrid that I didn't really want
to go to the edge of the world just to see if there
was something there. I was hoping she'd say
the same, but she was looking forward to it.
Being one of the first people to ever set foot
in a new land would bring us more glory than
raiding ever could.

I agreed, but said I still wanted to stay behind
just in case all that stuff about the sea monster
was true. She pointed out that we'd both
pledged our loyalty to Leif, so we didn't really
have a choice anyway.

Oh yeah. I'd forgotten about that.

Seventeenth Day

Leif has just announced that his father will be joining our expedition. What is he thinking?

He says that they've put their differences behind them, and won't be discussing religion for the journey.

Like that's going to work. As soon as we get into any sort of trouble, Leif will be praying to his god, and Erik will be calling upon the Asgard ones, and it will turn into an argument so painful that we'll be wishing for a giant sea serpent to come along and eat us.

Chapter 6

A strange new land

Eighteenth Day

We have now set off for a place that might exist, or might have been imagined by someone who'd spent too long at sea.

We helped Leif carry the supplies of water and dried trout onto the boat this morning. We seemed to have enough, though it's hard to judge when you don't know how far you're going.

Erik didn't join us after all. He fell off his horse this morning, hurt his foot and took it as a sign that he shouldn't go.

The crew pretended to be sorry about this, but I could tell that everyone was relieved to be avoiding the inevitable family tiffs.

So now we are sailing towards the empty horizon in the hope that somewhere will eventually appear. All I wanted was to join a raid. How did I end up here?

GET REAL

According to the account in the Saga of the Greenlanders, *written in the 14th century, Erik the Red intended to accompany his son Leif on his journey west from Greenland. But he changed his mind after falling from his horse just before the start of the expedition.*

Nineteenth Day

We have reached the end of the world. I can see it ahead of us, but no one will listen to me. There's a sheer drop and we're about to fall off. Why won't they act? It's as if they can't hear me.

Twentieth Day

Jörmangundr the sea serpent is here. It has slimy green scales, fiery red eyes and sharp fangs that swirl thick trails of venom into the dark sea. Look at it biting its own writhing tail!

We must return and tell the others never to venture this far west. Human eyes must never suffer this again.

Twenty-First Day

It's too late. The huge serpent has released its tail, and its poison is gushing into the sea. Toxic waves are washing over us, and soon we will all be dead. Then it shall coil and writhe onto land, and spew its foulness into the air. It is Ragnarok, the end of all things! The world will be destroyed!

Twenty–Second Day

I would like to apologise for my entries over the last few days. I should make it clear that we didn't sail over the edge of the world, or wake a giant serpent, or trigger the apocalypse. I was in fact suffering from a fever after a bout of very cold rain, and I imagined a lot of weird stuff. Astrid has been giving me plenty of fish and water, and I feel much better now.

Twenty–Third Day

There was a thick fog this morning and I found myself standing at the front of the ship, staring into it. It was as if the sea had risen and we were sailing through the clouds.

A gap appeared and I spotted a wide brown mass on the horizon. I was so hypnotised by the fog that I didn't fully understand what I was seeing. But then it struck me. This was it. This was land. We had found the new world we were searching for.

I called the others over, but the mist rolled back as soon as they came. I told them what I'd seen, but they assumed my fever had returned.

Minutes later, a sharp rock appeared from the fog, and the crew had to grab their oars and row frantically away. They wished they'd listened to me then.

We can't go any further until the weather improves, but it looks like Bjarni was telling the truth after all. There really is an amazing new land out here.

Twenty–Fourth Day

Actually, this new land isn't all that amazing. When the fog lifted early this morning, we could see a flat expanse of grey stones that led to some ice-capped mountains in the far distance. Leif told the crew to stay on board, but let me and Astrid go off and investigate with him.

We had to splash down into freezing water with small chunks of ice floating in it, and clamber onto a low, flat rock. The weak sun didn't warm me up much, so I had to hop from foot to foot just to stop myself going blue.

Leif crouched down, felt the rock with his hands and declared that the land would never be right for settling. Then we splashed back through the icy water.

Leif has named the place 'Helluland', instead of my suggestion 'Halfdanland' or Astrid's suggestion 'Astridland'.

143

We sail on.

GET REAL

According to the Saga of the Greenlanders, *the first land that Leif Erikson came to was called 'Helluland', which means 'land of flat stones'. Many scholars think this was the place we now call Baffin Island, which is part of Canada.*

Twenty-Fifth Day

We are sailing south, keeping close to the shore of this sparse new land. It goes on for miles, with the same flat rocks and faraway peaks. Now that we've discovered a new place, I think we should go back and tell everyone, but Leif is determined to find somewhere suitable for a new colony. And unless we fancy living on an unsheltered rock and eating ice, we haven't done that yet.

Twenty—Sixth Day

We saw some weird creatures on the rocks
today. They looked like foxes, but had thick
white fur and large, dark eyes. Astrid wanted to
take one as a pet and call it Fluffy. Leif wanted
to kill one and make a new hat. Luckily, we
didn't have time to stop.

Twenty—Seventh Day

We have crossed another stretch of open sea, and found another new land. Instead of flat stones, this one has shores of white sand leading to dense woodlands. We rowed the ship up to one of the beaches, and this time Leif let us all get out.

Some of the crew set about refilling our water, whilst others waded into the cold sea and caught some cod.

Leif and the others are sleeping on the shore tonight, but Astrid and I have chosen to come back to the ship. First, she frightened me by saying there might be bears in the forest. Then I frightened her by saying that, seeing as though no one had ever been there before, there could even be giants or dark elves. We both screamed and fled back here.

Twenty—Eighth Day

Leif has decided to move on again. He's convinced we're being guided to an even better place, and he won't stop until we get there. I was annoyed that this will put back my journey home for even longer, but I don't mind getting away from those thick woods and all the weird stuff that might be lurking in them.

Leif said the trees would make great timber, and it would be a handy place for Greenlanders to bring their cargo ships. He has decided to call it 'Markland'.

GET REAL

The second stop that Leif made, according to the Saga of the Greenlanders, *was named 'Markland', meaning 'wood land'. No one is sure where it was, but some believe it to have been on Canada's Labrador coast.*

Twenty—Ninth Day

We are out at sea again. The land with the forests is behind us and there is a strong wind in our sails. Leif is convinced it's transporting us to the place he's been searching for, though I wouldn't be too upset if it blew us all the way back home instead.

Thirtieth Day

Leif might have been right after all. Today we found a land with green hills rising above sandy beaches. Leif got out alone this time and strolled around on the grass. The clouds moved away as he was doing so, and bright sunlight shone on him, which he took as a further sign that we were heading in the right direction. When he came back, he told the crew to row us up an estuary.

First Day of the New Moon

Finally, Leif has found somewhere he's happy with.

The river led us to a large lake, and we got out and pulled the boat onto the shore. There was a flat meadow beyond, and past that a thick forest.

Some of the crew caught and cooked salmon for us, whilst Astrid gathered berries from the edge of the woods. Leif declared it was a wonderful meal, and a sign that we'd found the right place for our new settlement.

I was expecting we'd get a few days off after all that travel, but Leif told us to start building right away.

The crew grabbed their axes and made for the trees. I was hoping there would be a spare one for me, but there wasn't. I grabbed a knife instead, and decided to make do with that.

Leif strode into the forest, slapping the trunks of the trees, and declaring them to be good quality. Then the crew set to work with amazing speed, stripping the bark around the bottom of the trees, cutting V-shapes into their sides, pushing them over and getting out of

150

the way before they crashed to the ground in a cloud of dirt.

I chose a sturdy tree and began to slice it with the knife. It was difficult to make progress without an axe, but I thought it would show I had a good attitude if I tried anyway.

Soon all the trees around me had fallen, whilst I'd only managed to carve a shallow groove around mine. I gave it a shove, just in case, but it stood firm.

I stepped back, stretched out my aching arm and told the others they could finish it for me. They ignored my groove, and went about removing the bark from the base just like they'd done with the others.

Second Day

Astrid suggested that I leave the crew to cut down the trees and help her look for berries deeper in the woods. It was another bright day, so I managed to put all the thoughts of bears and dark elves out of my head.

We found some plants with long, winding stems and dark grapes, and gathered them into a cloth bag.

A wide grin spread across Leif's face when he saw them. He said they would be perfect for wine, which would be useful for the long winter nights.

I hope that wasn't his way of telling us he's planning on staying here until the end of next winter. I've already been missing for two months. I don't want to add an extra year onto that.

Leif gathered the crew and showed them the grapes, and they cheered. He said this place would be called 'Vinland' because of the wine it would provide.

GET REAL

Leif Erikson's third stop in The Saga of the Greenlanders *was 'Vinland'. Viking experts can't agree exactly where it was, though many believe it to have been Newfoundland in Canada.*

Third Day

Leif is really excited about this place. He says it's much farther south than Greenland or Iceland, and although the days will be shorter in summer, they will also be longer in winter. This will make it a much more pleasant place to live. It also means the grass won't wither in winter, so we can keep cattle outside all through the year.

He looked inland and said this new country could go on forever as far as we knew. It could become a new world, with even bigger towns than the ones we knew back home.

I thought he was getting a little carried away. Let's get our little settlement sorted first, then we can start dreaming about the vast distance beyond it.

Fourth Day

The crew have dragged the felled trees to the meadow beside the lake and are beginning to construct the first buildings of our settlement. Some of them are sawing wood, others are constructing timber frames and others are digging the turf to place on them.

I offered to help make the frames, and mentioned that I had plenty of wood-carving experience, but they weren't interested.

Leif said I should go back into the forest with Astrid and collect more grapes, so they could celebrate with wine when the buildings were finally finished.

We wandered back into the trees, and found the same patch of vines. Astrid insisted on going deeper into the wood so we could give Leif a full report about what was growing there.

We ventured past the area with the felled trees and into a part that was covered in lots of low, tangled plants.

Astrid said that none of the others had come this far into the forest before. That meant no

one had been as far west as us ever, which was pretty exciting.

I agreed that it made us the best explorers ever, but then I started to worry about what might be out here. If no one had ever been this way before, there could be anything lurking behind the trees.

One cold winter evening, Dad told me about the draugr, who are dead bodies that come back to life and attack the living. They are very stinky and very strong, and can grow until they're large enough to swallow you whole.

I told myself not to think about such horrid things, but then dark grey clouds gathered overhead, and it became harder to put them out of my mind. The forest became gloomier, as if we'd stayed out too late in the evening.

I said we should turn back, but Astrid said we shouldn't let bad weather put us off. I wanted to explain that I was more afraid of giant undead beasts, but I didn't want her to worry as well.

My legs felt unsteady and sweat was running down my temples. Astrid strode ahead. I called for her to stay back, but she didn't hear me.

Rain fell. The branches above us kept most of it off, but every so often a big drop would fall onto my face.

A blob of water rolled into my eyes. I tried to blink it out and my vision became blurry.

I could see something moving ahead of us – a shape flitting between trees. My pulse raced and my throat was dry. I wasn't imagining it this time. This was real. I'd disturbed a vengeful corpse and now it was coming for me.

I rubbed the rain out of my eyes and things became clear again. I couldn't see the figure anymore, but I could hear it, breathing and stepping on twigs as it paced around the trees.

I begged the creature not to grow bigger and swallow me. Then I ran back towards the lake. I tripped over a tangle of branches and crashed down to the ground. I was sure the monster was behind me, with its jaws expanding and its teeth extending into sharp points.

But I managed to scrabble up and make it out of the woods. It took me ages to get my breath back and tell the others what I'd seen.

Leif burst out laughing, though some of the crew exchanged nervous glances. Astrid emerged a few minutes later, and when I told her what had happened, she said she hadn't seen a thing.

Leif said I was obviously letting my imagination run away with me, and told the others to ignore me and get back to work.

GET REAL

The draugr were undead beings who featured in some Viking sagas. They were stinky, swollen corpses with super-strength who guarded treasure and got revenge on whoever had wronged them in life.

Chapter 7

Meeting the locals

Fifth Day

Last night some of the crew approached me when Leif wasn't around to check if I'd been telling the truth. I told them I had.

This morning several of them announced that they wanted to abandon this settlement and find somewhere without any living dead nearby.

Leif said they were being ridiculous, and we needed to settle the whole matter right away. He told me to lead them to the spot where I'd seen the creature so he could investigate.

We set off into the woods, with the crew following behind, holding up their axes and shields. I don't know what use they thought they were going to be. The draugr would just eat their weapons too.

It was hard for me to locate the exact place again, but eventually I recognised the branch I'd tripped over, and reckoned the encounter must have happened a few paces beyond.

Leif strode ahead, but then came to a stop. He hissed at us to be quiet. There was something moving. A figure was creeping around the trees. The others were gazing at it with open mouths and wide eyes.

I was slightly relieved that I hadn't been imagining it after all, but mostly terrified of being eaten. I scuttled back behind the others, reckoning that the creature might swallow them first and give me time to get away.

Leif inched forward. It was quite brave of him. I'd have sent one of the others out to meet the monster instead.

As he went on, he did something very strange. He dropped his axe and shield. I could see they wouldn't be much use against a super-strong corpse, but why get rid of them?

He went further, making a slow, beckoning gesture to the monster.

The figure emerged from the gloom. It was short, with dark eyes and long black hair. Now I could see it properly, it was obvious this wasn't a monster at all, but a human.

It was a man who was wearing trousers made from animal hide. He looked at Leif, who held his hands up to show he had no weapons, and then over at us. He made a nodding gesture and sank back into the forest. Leif told us the man must be one of the native peoples of this land.

On the way back, the others teased me for thinking I'd seen a genuine monster. I don't remember them being so casual about it on the way there.

Sixth Day

Now that my panic has gone, I'm a little disappointed I didn't see an actual monster. And I'm even more disappointed that we weren't the first people here after all. I wonder if the natives have been here forever?

Seventh Day

The native ventured into our settlement this morning, and brought four friends with him. They were all a similar height to him, at least a foot shorter than Leif and the others.

Some of the crew thought we were under
attack, and grabbed their axes, but Leif told
them to hold off. The natives were carrying
piles of animal pelts rather than weapons, so
they wanted to trade rather than fight.

The natives laid their pelts out and beckoned us over to look at them. From the gestures they made, they seemed to want some of our spears and axes in return, but Leif refused. Only the stupidest explorer would swap their axe for a pelt, so that the other person could chop them up with the axe and take the pelt back.

Leif went to the ship and returned with a roll of red wool, and the natives examined it before accepting it and leaving the skins.

Leif said that they seemed friendly, but we should be wary of them, especially during the winter months.

I need to talk to him about all this winter stuff. We've done plenty of exploring. Isn't it time to go back?

Eighth Day

Our settlement is finally complete. A row of three long huts with turf-covered roofs now look down onto the clear lake. The first bucket of wine was ready too, so there was lots of rowdy shouting and singing to celebrate.

Ninth Day

I spotted Leif on the shore this morning, gazing out across the lake with his hands planted on his hips. He was on his own for once, so I thought it would be a good chance to ask when we were going home.

I tapped him on the shoulder and said I wanted to talk about what would happen next. He grinned and said that he knew what I was going to ask.

He said I must have guessed he was planning on sailing back to Greenland soon to gather more people. And obviously I would want to know if Astrid and I could rule the colony whilst he was away. And the answer was yes.

This threw me so much that I forgot everything I'd planned to say. I staggered off to tell Astrid that we could be the temporary king and queen of Vinland and she was overjoyed.

Lots of odd things have happened since we left home, but being offered a chance to become a king has got to be the strangest.

Tenth Day

Although being a king would be amazing, I've decided I still want to go back. I've been very lucky to travel this far and see so many new things without getting eaten by sea monsters or dead people. But I've had enough for now. Maybe one day I'll return here and help Leif with the colony, but I need to go back to normal life for a while. Also, I'm scared that the natives will attack when Leif is away, and we'll be in charge of fighting them off.

I told Astrid, and she said I was right, and it was probably for the best, as our parents must be worried about where we are. I could tell that she was disappointed about not getting to be a queen, though.

Eleventh Day

Today we told Leif about our decision. He said he understood, but he still wanted to thank us for supporting him in Iceland and Greenland, so he was going to make us king and queen for the day.

He made special chairs for us from the storage boxes and had the crew bring us salmon and grapes. We spent the day thinking of all the things we could command everyone to do, like build a hall as long as seven houses, or have a feast in our honour every day for a year.

Being a real ruler would be much harder, of course. You'd spend so much time solving petty disputes and making sure no one used up the winter supplies, that you'd never have time to sit on a big chair and make ridiculous demands.

Twelfth Day

We are back at sea, sailing north up the coast so we can cross over to Greenland. We're going to stop there for a few days whilst Leif tells everyone about Vinland, then he's going to take us all the way home, just as he promised.

Eighteenth Day

We're back in Greenland now. Everyone wants to know all about Vinland, and Astrid and I have been answering questions all day. It's only a few weeks since I arrived here and marvelled at how these brave folks had made a home on the very edge of the world. Now I know it isn't the edge of the world, and we're seen as the brave ones.

Twenty—Ninth Day

Back home at last.

We arrived this afternoon. We leapt into the waves whilst Leif and the crew were still pushing the ship to the shore, and staggered to the village. It was exactly as we'd left it, except that Birger's roof had been fixed.

A crowd soon gathered and yelped questions at us. Dad and Mum pushed their way through, followed by Frode.

Dad glared at me with his face turning purple and his fists clenching into balls. He exploded into a rant about how I ran off with the raiders when I was meant to be working to earn enough money for Birger's roof.

Frode joined in, yelling about how Astrid had not only left without his permission, but also stolen his shields and axes before doing so.

Astrid took out her bag of coins and gave some to her dad to pay for the weapons, and some to my dad to pay for the roof. They both examined the coins briefly before returning to their shouting. Then Birger appeared and told everyone to get back to work.

Leif came over and stood next to us, whilst his crew gathered behind him.

He announced that he was Leif, son of Erik the Red. His voice boomed above the yapping of the crowd, and they fell silent.

He slapped me and Astrid on the back, and said everyone ought to be careful how they spoke to us, as we were now the former king and queen of Vinland.

The questions started up again. Everyone wanted to know what Vinland was, why it needed a king and queen, and why on earth anyone would choose us.

Leif said we would tell them everything, once they'd served a great feast in our honour.

Astonishingly, everyone agreed, including Birger. It must be great to have a voice so commanding that complete strangers will obey your wishes.

The others wandered away, whilst Leif told Dad, Mum and Frode about our amazing deeds. It struck me that last time I was standing on this stretch of grass, everyone was laughing at me for failing the tasks I had been set. Now I was returning as a hero.

First Day of the New Moon

Our feast carried on long into the night, and I woke up late this morning. We had pork, mutton, bread, carrots, cabbage and leeks, followed by an oatcake, apples and blueberries.

After the meal, Leif gave a long speech about how we'd crossed the ocean and discovered two new lands, before founding Vinland. He hopes it will grow to be even bigger than Iceland and Greenland one day, and said that everyone was welcome to join it. And if they did, they should never forget the names of Halfdan the Intrepid and Astrid the Fearless.

It's not too long since I wanted to be called Halfdan Skull-splitter, and renowned for my ruthless raiding skills. But raiding didn't turn out to be much fun. What's so great about stealing stuff from people who are weaker than you anyway?

Exploring, on the other hand, is much more impressive. We sailed further than anyone had gone before. We discovered new lands beyond the edge of the world. And we even met people that nobody knew existed. Now that's truly something to be proud of.

The End

The Vikings in North America

We use the term 'Viking' to refer to the people who lived in Denmark, Norway and Sweden in the 8th to 11th centuries. The word was once used for the pirates who sailed out to violently attack and steal from others. But we also use it for the more peaceful people from these countries too.

The Vikings were traders and explorers as well as fighters. They were farmers, who tended land and kept animals. They were craftsmen, who were skilled at working with metal and wood. And they were traders, who gathered silver, jewellery and pottery from around the world.

There is no doubt that the Vikings could be extremely violent, but violence was common in their era. So why are the Vikings remembered for being particularly bloodthirsty?

It's partly because the written evidence we have about them is biased. The Vikings raided churches and monasteries, and the accounts written by their victims describe them as savage and terrible.

But it's also because our notions of Vikings were formed long after their era. The image of the bare-chested warrior with the horned helmet was created in the writing and art of the 19th century.

The Viking Age is said to have begun in 793 AD, with the first raids on England. It continued until 1066 AD, with the defeat of the Norwegian King Harald Hardrada by the Saxon King Harold Godwinson.

The sophisticated longships and knarrs of the Vikings let them launch quick and brutal raids, and also allowed them to travel great distances for trading, with some reaching the Mediterranean and others venturing far down Russian rivers.

The ships allowed them to venture to Iceland and Greenland to set up new colonies, and even reach North America. The excavation of a Viking site in Newfoundland in the 1960s sparked interest in their exploration of the area, which took place nearly 500 years before the famous voyage of Christopher Columbus.

According to the *Saga of the Greenlanders*, Leif Erikson and his crew sailed from Greenland and came upon places he named 'stone-slab land', 'wood land' and 'vineland'.

The Vikings never managed to settle in North America, partly because of conflict with the native peoples. But the fact that they managed to get so far away from home is a testament to their great thirst for exploration.

How do we know about the Vikings?

How do we know about the Viking age,
when it happened so long ago?

The truth is that much of the written
evidence we have about the Vikings was
written by others. These were often their
enemies, so the accounts could be unreliable.

But the Vikings did have their own form
of lettering, known as 'Runes'. These were
usually carved in wood or stone, and used
for short pieces of writing.

There are also inscriptions and images

on coins that can help us to learn about them. Other objects such as weapons, jewellery and household utensils have been found. Chests of buried treasure from the era have even been unearthed.

Some Vikings were buried in their ships, along with their belongings, and locating these sites can be incredibly useful. Archaeologists now use radar to help discover them.

We can learn a lot about Vikings from their sagas. These were epic stories about things like voyages, rulers and feuds. The Vikings told these stories to each other, and they were eventually written down, although not until long after the events described in them had happened.

The most important ones for learning
about Viking exploration beyond
Greenland are the *Saga of Erik the Red*
and the *Saga of the Greenlanders*. They
don't agree on the details, but they both
describe how Leif Erikson found new lands
in what is now North America.

There was little evidence to back up these
accounts until the 1960s, when a team of
archaeologists discovered a Norse site on
the island of Newfoundland. The remains
of eight buildings, thought to be houses
and workshops, were found.

Timeline

793 AD

Viking raiders attack the abbey on Lindisfarne, off the coast of northern England. This date is seen as the start of the Viking Age.

795 AD

Vikings raid the monastery on Iona, off the west coast of Scotland.

841 AD

Vikings travel up the river Seine and attack the French town of Rouen.

845 AD

King Charles the Bald offers the Vikings a payment in silver to stop them attacking Paris. They begin to demand similar bribes elsewhere.

Timeline

865 AD

Viking forces land in Britain, seize land and eventually begin to settle.

c.874 AD

A colony is founded on Iceland.

878 AD

King Alfred of Wessex, later known as 'Alfred the Great', is victorious against the Vikings at the Battle of Edington. He draws up a treaty, in which the area controlled by the Vikings is known as the 'Danelaw'.

911 AD

Viking chieftain Rollo establishes a kingdom in France, becoming the first ruler of Normandy.

Timeline

980s AD

Vikings launch a series of fierce raids on England, during the reign of Aethelred the Unready.

c.982 AD

Erik the Red is exiled from Iceland and explores Greenland. He soon returns to set up a colony there.

c.1000 AD

Leif Erikson voyages to North America.

c.1030 AD

The colony in Vinland is abandoned.

1066 AD

King Harald Hadrada is killed at the Battle

Timeline

of Stamford Bridge, near York in northern England. The date is seen as the end of the Viking Age.

c.1230 AD

Snorri Sturluson writes *Heimskringla*, a history of the Norwegian kings. This and other 'kings' sagas' give us the story of the Vikings from their point of view, but they were written too long after the events recorded to be reliable.

15th century AD

The Viking settlement on Greenland disappears in mysterious circumstances. Could disease have wiped them out? Did they perish in a conflict with the Inuit people? We don't know.

Viking Hall of Fame

Egill Skallagrímsson
(c.910–c.990)

The hero of *Egil's Saga*, which was written in the 13th century. He is described as a warrior and a poet, capable of both bloody violence and artistic expression. It's said that he composed his first poem at the age of three, and killed his first enemy at the age of seven. If you ran into him, you'd have to hope you caught him in a poetic mood, rather than a murderous one.

Eric Bloodaxe
(c.885–954)

Norwegian who served as both King of Norway and Northumbria in northern England, and whose violent nickname has made him one of the best-known Vikings.

Viking Hall of Fame

According to the sagas, he killed his brothers in an attempt to retain power, which might explain his name. But we have no idea if this really happened, or if he was even called by the name at all in his lifetime.

Erik the Red (c.950–c.1003)

Viking explorer who's thought to have founded the first settlement in Greenland. According to the sagas, he first explored the land whilst he was exiled from Iceland for murder. He eventually returned to Iceland and convinced people to start the new colony with him.

Viking Hall of Fame

Freydís Eiríksdóttir
(born c.970)

The daughter of Erik the Red, who was described as a fearless warrior. In the *Saga of the Greenlanders*, it's said she set off on an expedition to Vinland once her brother Leif had returned. However, she got into a dispute with some of her fellow settlers and ended up killing them.

Gudrid Thorbjarnardóttir

Viking explorer who features in the *Saga of the Greenlanders*. It's said she travelled to Vinland with her husband Thorfinn Karlsefni, shortly after Leif Erikson's voyage. Whilst they were there, the couple had a son, Snorri Thorfinnsson. If the account is correct, it would make Snorri the first baby born to a European in North America.

Viking Hall of Fame

Harald Bluetooth
(c.910 ~ c.988)

Danish King who united different tribes into
a single kingdom. He fought wars against the
Germans, and converted to Christianity. In
1997, a method of exchanging data between
devices, and therefore uniting them, was
named after him. You can find the runic
Bluetooth logo on phones and computers.

195

Viking Hall of Fame

Harald Hardrada
(c.1015 – 1066)

Norwegian king whose name translates as 'hard ruler'. His reign came at the very end of what we class as the 'Viking Age'. In 1066, he attempted to invade England, but was thwarted by King Harold's forces at the Battle of Stamford Bridge. Harald Hardrada was killed by an arrow to the neck, but King Harold's victory turned out to be short-lived. He was defeated just a few weeks later by William the Conqueror at the Battle of Hastings.

Viking Hall of Fame

Ivar the Boneless
(died c.870)

Viking leader who invaded England, supposedly to get revenge for the killing of his father Ragnar Lothbrok. According to legend, he was so ruthless that he executed his enemies using the 'blood eagle', a gruesome method of killing in which the ribcage is opened and the lungs are pulled out so they resemble a pair of wings.

Lagertha

According to the Danish historian Saxo Grammaticus, who wrote in the 12th century, Lagertha was a fearsome warrior and the wife of the famous Ragnar Lothbrok. Saxo describes how she fought alongside the bravest men with her hair flowing loose around her shoulders. She may well have been fictional, but her story was remembered by generations of Vikings.

Viking Hall of Fame

Leif Erikson

Viking explorer who's thought to have been the first European to visit North America. According to the sagas, he established a settlement at Vinland, which could be Newfoundland in Canada. So whilst some may believe that Christopher Columbus was the first European to 'discover' America in the year 1492 AD, there is plenty of evidence that the Vikings were there first.

Viking Hall of Fame

Ragnar Lothbrok

Legendary warrior who lived in the 9th century, and features in Norse poetry and sagas. He's said to have launched vicious attacks against England and the Holy Roman Empire, and to have died when he was cast into a snake pit by the King of Northumbria. Historians now doubt whether he really existed at all, but his name lives on as the ideal of the fearless Viking.

Snorri Sturluson (1179–1241)

Icelandic clan chieftain who wrote narratives of Norse mythology and sagas about Viking kings. He was writing centuries after the events he described, so we can't take his work to be accurate, but it has shaped our idea of the Vikings for centuries.

Glossary

Adze
A tool with a sharp blade at the end that's used for shaping wood. It looks like a miniature axe.

Archaeologist
Someone who studies the remains of ancient civilisations.

Asgard
The realm of the gods in Viking mythology.

Bifrost
A burning rainbow bridge that connects the world of humans to the world of gods in Viking mythology.

Boss
A round piece of metal in the centre of a shield that's used to deflect blows from weapons.

Clinker
A method of boat building in which the edges of planks overlap each other.

Colony
A group of people who leave their country to form a settlement in a new one.

Draugr
Hideous corpses that have come back to life, in Viking mythology.

Fjord
A long and narrow body of water that reaches inland from the sea.

Jörmungandr
A sea serpent that circled the realm of humans, in Viking mythology.

Glossary

Knarr
A type of ship used by the Vikings to carry cargo. They were wider and deeper than longships, and had a taller mast and a bigger sail.

Longship
A type of ship used by the Vikings for sea voyages and raids. They were also narrow enough to be rowed down rivers.

Glossary

Midgard
The realm where humans lived in Viking mythology. It was also known as 'Middle Earth'.

Norse
A term used to refer to the Scandinavian people in ancient or medieval times.

Northmen
Another term for Vikings.

Parchment
An animal skin that has been stretched and smoothed so it can be written on.

Plunder
To steal goods violently from somewhere, in a war or a raid.

Ragnarok
The great battle in Viking mythology that would destroy the world.

Runes
The letters used by the Vikings. They were made from straight lines, which made them easy to carve on stone or wood.

Saga
Entertaining tales that the Vikings told to each other, that were later written down.

THE LONG-LOST SECRET DIARY OF THE WORLD'S WORST

**The Long-Lost Secret Diary
of the World's Worst Samurai**
Shortlisted for the 2020–2021 Spark!
Kingston and Richmond Children's Book Awards

**The Long-Lost Secret Diary
of the World's Worst Astronaut**
Chosen for the 2019 Summer
Reading Challenge.

*'Although easy to read, the vocabulary
is great and the plot lines engaging –
excellent reads for developing readers.'*
Library Girl and Book Boy Blog

Tim Collins / Sarah Horne

PB ISBN: 978-1-912233-19-9

Tim Collins / Sarah Horne

PB ISBN: 978-1-912233-20-5

Tim Collins / Isobel Lundie

PB ISBN: 978-1-912537-26-6

Tim Collins / Sarah Horne

PB ISBN: 978-1-912006-67-0

Tim Collins/ Sarah Horne

PB ISBN: 978-1-912006-66-3

Tim Collins / Isobel Lundie

PB ISBN: 978-1-912537-44-0

Tim Collins / Isobel Lundie

PB ISBN: 978-1-913337-17-9

Tim Collins / Isobel Lundie

PB ISBN: 978-1-912904-66-2

Tim Collins / Isobel Lundie

PB ISBN: 978-1-912904-94-5

Tim Collins / Isobel Lundie

PB ISBN: 978-1-913971-04-5

Tim Collins / Isobel Lundie

PB ISBN: 978-1-913971-13-7

Tim Collins / Isobel Lundie

PB ISBN: 978-1-912904-23-5

A selected list of Scribo titles

The prices shown below are correct at the time of going to press. However, The Salariya Book Company reserves the right to show new retail prices on covers, which may differ from those previously advertised.

Gladiator School by Dan Scott

1	Blood Oath	978-1-908177-48-3	£6.99
2	Blood & Fire	978-1-908973-60-3	£6.99
3	Blood & Sand	978-1-909645-16-5	£6.99
4	Blood Vengeance	978-1-909645-62-2	£6.99
5	Blood & Thunder	978-1-910184-20-2	£6.99
6	Blood Justice	978-1-910184-43-1	£6.99

Iron Sky by Alex Woolf

1	Dread Eagle	978-1-909645-00-4	£9.99
2	Call of the Phoenix	978-1-910184-87-5	£6.99

Children of the Nile by Alain Surget

1	Cleopatra must be Saved!	978-1-907184-73-4	£5.99
2	Caesar, Who's he?	978-1-907184-74-1	£5.99
3	Prisoners in the Pyramid	978-1-909645-59-2	£5.99
4	Danger at the Circus!	978-1-909645-60-8	£5.99

Ballet School by Fiona Macdonald
1. Peter & The Wolf   978-1-911242-37-6   £6.99
2. Samira's Garden   978-1-912006-62-5   £6.99

Aldo Moon by Alex Woolf
1 Aldo Moon and the Ghost
    at Gravewood Hall   978-1-908177-84-1   £6.99

The Shakespeare Plot by Alex Woolf
1 Assassin's Code   978-1-911242-38-3   £9.99
2 The Dark Forest   978-1-912006-95-3   £9.99
3 The Powder Treason   978-1-912006-33-5   £9.99

Visit our website at:

www.salariya.com

All Scribo and Salariya Book Company titles can be
ordered from your local bookshop, or by post from:

The Salariya Book Co. Ltd,
25 Marlborough Place
Brighton
BN1 1UB